CW00409323

The Bully Tell-Off

THE IDEA

Acknowledgements

Thank you to my friends Muhummad, Folarin and Charlie for letting me interview them even when they could have been doing something more interesting or fun.

My teacher, Miss Marcella Robb for always encouraging me to write, I am truly grateful.

For my sister, Sophia.

Chapter One

It's been a bit tough at school these days. Apparently, there had been a super-secret meeting amongst the teachers after the new kid got bullied and ended up in the hospital.

I imagine the meeting was held in the headteacher's office and that was when they came up with a bully report system. With this system, a large box with an opening, making it look like an ugly piggybank was placed outside the playground.

The idea was that students who were being bullied but weren't brave enough to tell anyone about it could slip in a note reporting their bullies, and with whatever information they gave, the school could do something about it.

No offence to our headteacher, Mr William, but I just couldn't picture him coming up with this idea. I could see him nodding along as they brainstormed.

Most of the kids in school were worried about the bullies finding out who reported them, and this could lead to them being bullied even more.

I wasn't bullied, not yet at least, maybe because I was rather tall for my age, but I knew some kids in my class who were being bullied daily and I doubt if any would tell the school about it.

BULLY REPORT

I think it's a brilliant idea and all, but it's obviously not working as during assembly, Mr William complained about us not taking it seriously, and mentioned how the report box is littered with chocolate and biscuit wraps, and even has gum stuck on it. Bullies have taken over the place!

When I come home to say how bad things have been and how perhaps mum should consider home-schooling me, she doesn't budge. She says school isn't just about learning, but a great way to make new friends and make better progress in life.

I don't think she's ever been bullied.

I had a few more things to say about the topic, but she was about to get on a zoom call at work and shooed me out of her room.

How rude!

My best friend's name is Tom. Well, Thomas. I guess everyone likes to shorten their name to sound cool.

Unless like me, your name is Jamal, then there isn't much you can do with it as no one wants to be called Jam…at least not me.

Thomas "Tom" Condron

Tom always yammers about the book he wrote last winter and gets all the attention. While I, seem like some kind of...well, someone that hasn't done anything, and everyone just leaves alone. The point is, I do have friends and my progress is just fine, but Tom was like a school sensation.

My older brother is Jake, Jake the trickster if you ask me. When mum tells us to clean the living-room, he says that he needs to make an urgent phone call or pretends to do something important, and I should go ahead and start without him.

But by the time I am done, I see him at the park, having the time of his life!

My little brother Jonah, or Jonah the
annoying like I call him, he scales the shelves
like spider man. Every time my teacher gives

us homework, I keep it on a high shelf to do it later. But when I get back, I see paint on the pages, and it seems like someone farted on it which I am sure they probably did, and I can only imagine Jonah did it.

Finally, our guard dog, Kim. Kim is actually just the family dog, but boy am I scared of that dog! Whenever I go to water the plants in the garden, I feel like Kim's going to crush me to bits, his huge jaws and the saliva constantly dripping doesn't help much. He gets bigger each day, and so do his bulging muscles. You'd think he went to a gym.

I have been thinking of telling mum that we should give him away because I am not sure the dog likes me either, I'm sure there's a relative who'd take him or maybe a nice shelter for scary dogs.

Then, I immediately feel guilty as Kim is part of the family, and I'm honestly terrified he might show up barking in my dreams if he knew of my plans.

I know I have been lazy lately…not entirely true as mum has always said I was lazy for as long as I can recall. Now I am beginning to believe her.

Let me paint a picture, we were given this homework at the beginning of the week, and I need to get it done before the end of the term or end up in summer school. I reach for it for the first time to see what the assignment really was about. When I looked, you would not believe how much I had to do, and I had not even started. Without shame, I went to ask mum for help. As soon as I mentioned homework, she starts laughing like a crazy person. I guess the stress from work is really getting to her. So, I just went along with it and moved on to asking Jake if he could help me instead.

He said he would, but it was going to cost me. I had no choice, so I said yes without even thinking.

But when I gave him the only £10 I had in this world, he ran like Sonic with his phone to his room, slammed the door and locked it.

From that experience, I learnt something at least. *Never give money to irresponsible people who will not do the job.*

April is my birthday month, but things are not off to a great start. There are more cases of bullying at school, I've lost £10, and the dog still doesn't like me. Maybe tomorrow will be better if I can get this assignment done.

THE BULLY REPORT

Name: ~~Aiden Condron~~

Class: Year 4, Kingfishers

~~I'm not sure, but I think I'm being bullied by my older brother.~~

Chapter Two

It wasn't easy falling asleep last night. And I know I dreamt a lot even though I can't really remember any of it. You can imagine how grumpy I felt, only to wake up to a note from mum that read,

Jamal,

I have been called in to have a conversation with your teacher.

If it is anything about failing math, you are grounded for the entire summer.

Love, Mum.

Yes, mum leaves little notes like this sometimes, so she doesn't forget, especially when she needs to get something from the shop before we wake up, or maybe it's just her way of creating suspense. She does read a lot of crime novels. Jake and I always joke about how she always signs off '*love mum*' even when you can tell she was angry when she scribbled.

Anyway, I knew I was in trouble as parents only got invited to school when it was parents' evening, you were getting an award or you had done something terrible. It wasn't parents evening, I hadn't won any award, so….

Mum and my teacher, Miss Damion finally had the talk about me, I was summoned from class to join them in the office. I had a feeling she was going to make me start summer school immediately just to punish me, but she did not. Instead, Miss Damion said that I needed more friends and even snitched on how I just sit there alone, most of the time. I have no idea what she is talking about because I play with Tom and his friends.

Even when I'm in no mood to talk and want to be alone, there's always that clueless classmate, complaining to me about Math or English like we aren't in the same class.

Few minutes in, Miss Damion still hadn't mentioned summer school, and I wondered if she had the wrong kid which would not be the first time, but…oh well, I still have my homework to complete before school's over.

I walked pass the bully report box as I went from the office to join my friends at the playground, only three weeks and it looked like it had been there for years.

I wonder if bullies looked at the box to see which of their prey would dare walk there and slide in a report.

I wondered also if the kids being bullied were also staring at the box and watching to see if their bullies were hanging around to see who would snitch.

I saw the little sister of one of my classmates crying by herself close to the basketball court, maybe she was being bullied or just crying because no one would play with her.

It really wasn't my business, if only I could find a quiet spot to complete my homework…

'Jamal! Over here!' I heard someone call out, I knew it was Tom even before I turned around. He asked me to come join them on the basketball court…maybe for a few minutes, I thought. I would complete the homework right after.

Of course, that did not happen, second homework I had failed to submit this term, this meant trouble.

THE BULLY REPORT

Name: W

Class: YEAR 5

There is a gang of kids my age pushing me around in my area.

They have ~~being~~ been doing this for months now, and it's getting really frustrating.

What do I do?

Chapter Three

I fantasized during assembly, that home-works in general would get cancelled. It's ridiculous, I know, but I hear this is the age for stuff like that. I could already see my classmates celebrating. But that will never happen because the teachers I know would have a rebellion (especially Mr Grey, who gives the most difficult assignments) and that would be bad for us kids. So, I can cross that from my list.

For some reason, Jonah has been all grumpy these days. He's stopped climbing shelves and doesn't leave behind a trail of bad smells and paint anymore. And the weirdest thing is, he plays with the dog which even dad is scared of but refuses to admit. I'm keeping the kick-out Kim idea though.

Anyway, Jonah is still struggling to talk as he hadn't even turned two yet, so, when I asked him if he was okay, I couldn't understand anything he babbled about. I did pick out 'Shhh!' though. It was loud and came out at the end of his mumbled sentence. I find it suspicious how he communicates better when he wants chicken and nuggets.

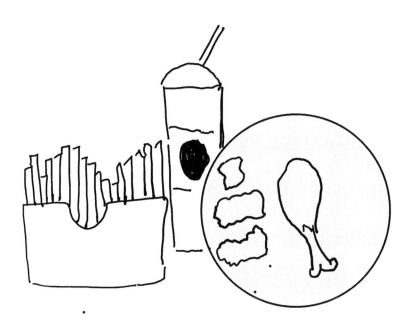

'Jonah is teething' Mum said to dad when they sat down in the evening to listen to the news or maybe she said he had the flu, I wasn't really paying attention. But she did say he was okay and didn't need to see the doctor.

Dad picked Jonah up and said something in his Nigerian accent, he usually does that when he is trying to get Jonah to laugh and calls him some pet names I never understand.

Then I heard my name being mentioned and froze for a second.

'…his teacher says he needs to mix up more with other kids, and that he is quite clever but chooses not to work at his studies.'

At least she said I was clever. Mum had nodded in agreement when Miss Damion had said 'chooses not to work' part because she did say I was lazy at home.

'It's just the age, he is only ten. We will help him focus more.' Dad said, he was usually too tired on a weekday for these conversations.

Just then Jonah saved the day by the stink I usually get upset about. He needed a diaper change and mum took him in while I slowly made my way upstairs to the room I shared with Jake.

When Jonah is Jake's age, I wonder about the things he'll do. But thankfully, I won't be home by then. I'll probably be in college or something, calling mum and dad regularly to check up on them.

THE BULLY REPORT

Name: anonymous

Class: guess! lol

THERE ARE NO BULLIES IN THIS SCHOOL!!!

Chapter Four

Today, the substitute teacher taught us something new. I wasn't listening very well, so I pretty much didn't know what to do about the math problems on my sheet. I asked one of my friends, who wasn't Thomas, (If you think the name of this other friend of mine is difficult to pronounce, you should try spelling it) but with the reply he gave, it not only made me reconsider our friendship, it made me want to switch seats.

Then I remembered I wasn't glued to my chair and could ask one of the smart kids. But they looked right through me and continued what they were doing. I didn't get mad. When you're that smart, you've earned the right to look through people and not respond to their questions. One of them even said I should listen, learn more and play less. People like that do not know what they're saying because I've learnt a lot on Minecraft and Roblox.

beep!

Speaking of Roblox, after school yesterday, I was considering items to buy for my game character, eating my snacks and minding my business, when mum walked in, assessed the situation, and told me I'd end up in summer school. She was tired of repeating herself and confiscating my video games. I was tired of the pattern too, but of course I didn't say it aloud. I just put on a sad face and tried to keep my tablet screen from going off. If you ask me, the blame should be on tech geniuses who create these addictive games and tablets. I tell you; I dream of certain game levels in my sleep!

I think the smart kid's advice got to me. During lunch break, I don't join Thomas in talking about the world Cup. I don't really care about football, but it seemed to make my dad happy when I watch with him, and it's not cool when everyone's talking about it and you have nothing to say. And it does make one feel like a grownup, discussing sports.

It's Thursday, which means *spaghetti* day at school dinner. I go over to where I always sit and find the new kid on my seat. He hadn't touched his food, and he seemed to have been crying.

"Are you okay?" I ask him, trying to remember his name. Was it Collin or Moses?

He's been away for weeks since the incident, and on the day he returned, a few of us had awkwardly gathered round him. Nadia had slipped him a note. She had a note for everything. Birthdays, dojo points, any achievement at all. Her handwriting was really neat, and next to a *happy birthday* or *congratulations,* she'd include a drawing. Now, her kindness will take her places, but I don't see her being an artist.

The new kid said he was okay. He said thank you and started eating his meal. At least I got him to eat, it felt awkward just watching him eat slowly,

I was about to walk away, but instead I sit beside him and ask 'what is your name, mine is Jamal'.

'My name is Adeola' he said quietly, and when I said it back to him, it didn't really sound the same. There was a bruise on his other cheek, and on the hand, he used to rub at it.

I felt sorry for him, so we ate quietly and talked about his old school a little bit.

I tried to get Thomas and the others to let him join our group, which they did reluctantly as someone said we were already too many in the group.

Adeola and his family had just moved two buildings away from mine and as we were in year five and lived really close to school our parents had given us permission to go home by ourselves like big kids. Adeola and I walked home together.

I was quite tall for a 10-year-old and Adeola was rather little for same age.

He later confided in me that he felt safer walking home with me. If only he knew how fast, I would run if we were attacked by older kids.

The bully reports seemed to have stopped coming in or the teachers just stopped talking about them.

School continued with the bullies and the bullied all taking their place in the circle of life...well, that's what they called it in Disney's Lion Guard.

THE BULLY REPORT

Name:

Class:

I'm new here and most of my classmates tease me about my accent.

Chapter Five

Today was the last day before our 6-week summer holiday. Most people in my class seemed to have figured out what they planned to do.

Some had travel plans with their parents, some were going to one camp or the other, my family had none planned as my mum said we had spent all the money travelling a few months before for my uncle's wedding in Lagos. So, games are the only thing I can say to people when asked how I intend spending my holiday. Until now…

I returned from school that Thursday, I must have seemed genuinely sad because mum told Jonah and Jake to leave the room and asked what was wrong. She asked if it was about her plan to register me for summer school, and seemed surprised when I told her it wasn't. I told her about Adeola, and the first thing that woman did, was correct my pronunciation!

'It is a Nigerian name, not English Jamal!' she laughed.

She was also quite impressed by my concern, which was a little offensive, because I've always been a kind person.

It was just that gaming and fending off my loud and annoying brothers took so much of my time I rarely got to show it. My brothers can be so annoying.

She mentioned how bullying was discussed during the previous parents-teachers meeting and asked if I wanted to do something about it.

'What could I possibly do, I can't fight off the bullies' I said with some panic in my voice,

Mum laughed again, she must have imagined me playing superhero and thought it ridiculous then said;

'I wasn't asking you to fight anyone dear, just wanted to know if you have any idea on how to help those who are bullied.'

I told her I would love to, but I hadn't quite figured out how.

Mum pushed for any idea I had, and I found myself rambling about how I couldn't exactly confront the Bully myself and how the school wasn't exactly finding it easy dealing with the situation.

Before I could mention that I didn't really think I could do much except be kind to Adeola and others who are being bullied, I thought of Thomas' book and told mum what if I wrote a book about it?

Now, I don't know exactly what mum does at work, but she immediately drew out a notepad and we started brainstorming. She was so excited about

the book idea; she started asking me all these questions. Maybe I should have just said I have no idea.

My daily two-hour slot for games and TV for the day was fast ticking, I did not like this at all.

Before I could properly respond, she handed me a new notebook and a pen, and told me to figure it all out and get back to her. If I could sell the idea, I'd work on the book instead of going to summer school.

Why didn't she say that sooner?

I guess this was better than summer school, so I started writing, and it didn't seem so bad. I may end up being famous for helping kids who were bullied, I guess I was kinder than mum knew.

THE BULLY REPORT

Name:

Class:

I don't like it here.

p.s bring back ms. Allen!

Chapter Six

Dad was in a rush, trying not to miss his flight, he was travelling for work which was quite rare. He'd forgotten something, so the Uber driver had to turn around. I didn't see what it was, but mum rushed out to give him the parcel outside. I waved through the window, hoping he'd see me, but he didn't.

Jake didn't even move from the sofa.

He had been mean to me earlier, and dad had scolded him. Now he sat in a corner eating strawberries and watching a horror movie on his tablet.

I could tell it was one of his vampire series by the sound of someone screaming, maybe I should go tell mum, so she takes away his tablet as I knew he wasn't allowed to watch those.

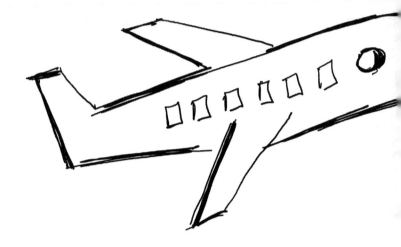

Since Jake was the only bully in my life, I decided to observe him. Being told-off by dad had really put him in a bad mood. I couldn't imagine what he'd do to me if I wrote a book about him or made it obvious. If I'm being honest, I couldn't see myself writing pages upon pages. Life of an author was a tough one, mum kept making me go back to write some things all over, how can she correct a story that is not even hers!

I thought of asking Thomas for help, but *nah!* he might accuse me of copying him and be all smug about it.

When she came in, mum asked me if I had made any real progress. She even stopped stirring her soup to look expectantly at me.

There's something about being put on the spot by mum. It's almost like there's an audience watching and a spotlight above me. I couldn't not say anything. I ramble about the book being a short story, and then I thought of Jake and told her we could call it "The Scolding of The Bullies." I throw in the word *epic,* so it sounds important.

She didn't seem impressed.

She said it was a brilliant idea to want to do something about bullying in my school through writing a book, but that I had to put more thought into it. She mentioned how I used a lot of big words when pitching my ideas to her, but that it was okay to sound and talk like the kid that I am, and it should show in my writing too. She also talked about how no one could really put a final stop to bullying, but what mattered was being kind and trying and listening... giving people a voice. She asked if I understood, and I did.

"You could call it *The Bully Report.*" She said, she didn't think the school would mind.

I thought it sounded too grown-up; I also didn't want the teachers thinking they gave me the idea. *No way!*

Also, listening to mum's little speech, it made sense that I come up with title and do it my way.

"How about *The Bully Tell-Off?*" I ask her, worried it sounded too childish.

Mum stood still for a few seconds, gently placed the soup spoon on a plate and hugged me.

'Sounds brilliant, Jamal.' she said 'absolutely brilliant!'

THE BULLY REPORT

Name:

Class:

~~My dad says everyone gets bullied, and to man up!~~

Chapter Seven

Today, I had swimming lesson. Mum wanted me to keep practicing, so I'd be great at it by the time school resumes. If I had to describe swimming, I would say terrible. We must dip our entire face inside the pool, splashing around in the pool but not excited about my head in water.

Also at school, everyone starts acting silly when the teachers aren't looking. Swimming was one of those activities I tried to convince mum to get me out of but failed so now I just try to enjoy it, splashing around and not being in class is not so bad.

She said I should be happy that I had the privilege to learn. When she was my age, she never had the opportunity. I wanted to tell her that she turned out fine but didn't want to risk getting told off for being rude instead I said a sulky *'thank you'*

To which mum responded by saying with that tone, I shouldn't have bothered.

When I got back from swimming, I thought I'd get back in mum's good book, by writing something instead of the usual gaming.

I've been googling on bully-related topics, and I couldn't wait for school to resume so I could speak to Adeola. He wasn't the chatty type, and I didn't expect him to tell me everything, but I knew talking with him would help in my research. I sound so grown up.

Then I remembered I had a few classmates who lived close by. I wish I had a phone so I could reach out to them, but I don't see my parents buying me a phone till I turn fifteen, maybe. Maybe when I write my book and have to talk to

other famous people mum would let me have my own phone…

Mum had a few of the mobile numbers of my friends' mums who lived near us and was happy to call them. She said we could make a list and I could stop by on one of our walks, and she'd pick me up later. She gave me a list of sensible questions to ask, and not to push if they didn't want to talk about the topic.

I just hope no one makes up a story about getting bullied, just to feature in the book. I really hoped those who agreed to share their story, would be honest. And when mum publishes it, and gives out copies to my classmates and teachers, I hope the

bullies feel ashamed of themselves. Just like Jake did after Dad told him off. Well, I hope he did.

THE BULLY REPORT

Name:

Class:

'm the bully. Come get me!

Chapter Eight

As usual, I got into a fight with Jake and Jonah. We had all run to the TV and tried to get the remote control Then, Jake said he saw mum switch the remote control and hid it in the room. I thought that was true. So, Jonah and I spent five minutes looking for the remote but after wasting our time, we knew it was a trick. Well, I knew it was a trick. Jonah gave up few seconds in and decided to draw with his colour pens instead. Or make marks, as they call it or whatever he did. They looked so silly, but mum always said they looked amazing.

Something new I just learnt about mum; she doesn't know anything about art.

Which is surprising, because she has lots of friends who are artists, and is always buying paintings.

Jake and I started arguing (*nothing new there*), and he roughed up my hair which he knew I hated. He even threatened to eat the chips I'd saved for later.

When mum and dad came home, I tried to explain why we hadn't showered and tidied up like they told us to, but here is what they said: "No time for that. Go shower and get ready for church."

This is why I throw a "Happy Goodbye Party" when they leave for the holidays, anniversary, and work trips. Maybe I should tell God about Jake and see if I could swap him for a nicer brother.

We all had to shower and dress up. The problem with that is that our house only has two bathrooms. And I know lots of people have just one, but we have Jake in our house and that complicates everything.

When we were ready, we hopped in dad's work van and rode to church. Church was really cool because we have our own classroom according to different ages, and the Sunday school teachers really have a way with telling bible stories. Oh, and there's snacks! Onion and cheese flavoured crisps, fruits, juice, cake and sometimes *Krispy crème* doughnuts.

There was even *jollof rice* when it was someone's birthday or a baby dedication, I hate to admit to mum but the rice from church tastes so much better than hers.

I can focus with Jake in the teenagers' classroom. The teenagers usually look miserable, like they don't want to be here And they all pretty much dress the same bu seem to think they look different. It's usually the same style of clothes, just differen colours and sizes.

Mum hopes Jonah will make friends and stop being so shy in public, since he's the opposite at home. His teacher is full of praises for him and doesn't believe us when we tell her how he behaves at home. Sometimes, she laughs but I don't think it's funny at all.

I thought that we would learn about the plagues in Egypt today, but we did not Instead, we were doing a drama practice fo

Easter. Drama or any form of play or acting wasn't really my thing. I'd think of anything o escape. performing in front of the congregation. So, imagine my expression when Uncle Chidi suggested I play the lead role of Jesus. Thankfully, Aunt Anne insisted I read and be the narrator instead, because I was the best reader in the class. We called all the teachers in church Uncle and Aunty out of respect.

I don't know for what exactly, but I should mention Aunty Anne in the acknowledgement section of my book for getting me out of acting. Mum can figure out the reason.

ACKNOWLEDGEMENT

I would like to thank Aunt Anne for ...

THE BULLY TELL-OFF

Name:

Class:

My step-brother bullies me. I don't see how the school can help.

And I don't want to get in trouble.

Chapter Nine

Jake was playing heavy metal when mum and I left the house. Jonah refused to join us on our walk because he was too busy drawing his dream house. Mum thought it looked like a luggage, and I thought it seemed more of a cake, so Jonah got angry, tore up the paper and started again. Mum tried to tell him it wasn't that bad, but I think she just didn't want to buy a new set of colour pencils so soon again.

When I have children, I will make sure they don't like heavy metal and stuff like that. Jake's a teenager, so he gets away with a lot of things. But he's not yet eighteen and can't afford a haircut without asking dad or mum for money, so I don't see why he gets to do as he likes.

I like when I get some time with just mum or dad, but I knew mum would find a way to discuss the book while on this walk.

First, we feed the ducks, then we take a walk to the new pier. The air is colder there, mum says.

Dad had talked about us going on the boat now that the pier was a few minutes' walk from us.

Soon, we'd all get on it and go somewhere fun at Central London. Any where's okay, all that matters is that we stop at Mc Donald's before heading back home.

On our way back, mum stops at the first person on my list; Nadia.

Nadia is one of the most brilliant people in my class, and she likes writing notes, so I know she would have something to say about my bully research.

We get to Nadia's house; mum tells me to knock. Lately, she's been encouraging my independence by letting me come home on my own, pay for groceries at the store when we go shopping for things she forgot to order online, or when we run out of ham, milk or bread. I even get to throw away the bin!

Let's just say things get chaotic when there's no toast in that house.

My heart is beating loudly, because I've been brainstorming and writing about *The Bully Tell-Off,* but now interviewing people would make it real, and that, I find intimidating.

I knock twice.

It's about time we told off those bullies!

THE BULLY TELL-OFF

(The Confrontation)

Daniel Chimezie Ngamdy

Illustrated by Obehi Aigiomawu

THE BULLY TELL-OFF

(The Confrontation)

Coming up with the idea of The Bully Tell-Off was quite easy. But now, it's time for Jamal to go through with his plan.

It's time for the bullied to confront their bullies... but how?

Have you got a bully report?

.

ABOUT THE AUTHOR

Daniel Chimezie Ngamdy, is a nine-year-old budding writer whose writing journey began with a love for reading, and at seven he put together a collection of some of his poems, and published when he turned eight. Deciding to try something different, he explored writing short stories, before taking it a step further by embarking on *The Bully Tell-Off* series.

Instagram: @daniel_writes0404

Printed in Great Britain
by Amazon

22547648R00057